MY FIRST WORDS:
ANIMALS
THE ILLUSTRATED A-Z GLOSSARY

This book belongs to:

....

....

WANDERLUST PRESS

A QUICK NOTE FOR THE ADULTS...

THANKS FOR PURCHASING THIS BOOK...
...we really hope you & your children enjoy it. If you have the chance, then all feedback on Amazon is greatly appreciated. We have put a lot of effort into making this book, so if you are not completely satisfied, please email us at benchinnock@hotmail.com and we will do our best to address any issues.

IS THIS BOOK MISPRINTED?
Printing presses, like humans, aren't quite perfect. Send us an email at benchinnock@hotmail.com with a photo of the misprint, and we will get another copy sent out to you!

CHECK OUT OTHERS IN THIS RANGE!
Our other A-Z glossary titles include:

- My First Words: FOOD (pictured to the right)
- My First Words: HOME
- My First Words: COLORS AND SHAPES
- My First Words: NATURE
- My First Words: DOWNTOWN
- My First Words: CLASSROOM

WANDERLUST PRESS

No part of this book may be copied, reproduced or sold without express permission from the owner.

Copyright Wanderlust Press 2021. All rights reserved.

Alligator

Antelope

Anaconda

Armadillo

Alpaca

Ant

Anteater

Insect

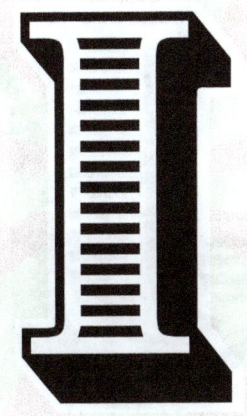

Iguana

Kangaroo

Killer Whale

K

Kookaburra

Koala

Komodo Dragon

Narwhal

Quail

Rabbit

Rhinoceros

Reindeer

Rooster

R

Rat

Rattlesnake

Rottweiler

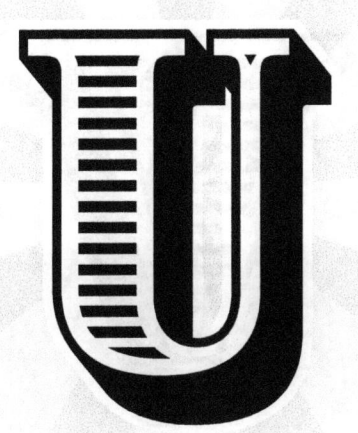

Vulture

Y

Yak

Zebra

www.ingramcontent.com/pod-product-compliance
Lightning Source LLC
Chambersburg PA
CBHW082106280426
43661CB00090B/907